# You Are What You Are

Modern Curriculum Press
BEGINNING
TO
READ
Series

# You Are What You Are.

by Valjean McLenighan

illustrated by Jack Reilly

## MODERN CURRICULUM PRESS
### Cleveland • Toronto

ISBN 0-8136-5581-1 (paperback)
ISBN 0-8136-5081-X (hardbound)

7 8 9 10          99 98 97

4

You do not look good in blue.

Look. Please stop. I can not help my good looks.

I see.

7

At the big house.

Hello. Did you put her away for good?

Yes.

Please do.

## You Are What You Are

**Valjean McLenighan,** author of several books in the MCP Beginning-To-Read Series, is a writer, editor, and producer.

**Uses of This Book:** Reading for fun, practice in appreciating characterization through humor. Children will enjoy this classic story, based on *Snow White and the Seven Dwarfs,* that they can read themselves.

**Word List:** All of the 79 words used in *You Are What You Are* are listed. Regular plurals and verb forms of words already on the list are not listed separately, but the endings are given in parentheses after the word.

| | | | | | | | |
|---|---|---|---|---|---|---|---|
| **1** | you | | away | **11** | oh | | yes |
| | are | | make(s) | | surprise | **14** | may |
| | what | | me | | kitten | | go |
| **4** | who | | blue(s) | **12** | ran | | now |
| | look(s) | **6** | not | | from | **15** | but |
| | good | | in | | big | | no |
| | do | | please | | how | **17** | find |
| | I | | stop | | funny | **19** | get |
| | thank(s) | | can | | for | | that |
| | know | | help | | your | **20** | happy |
| **5** | the | | my | | home | | birthday |
| | girl | | see | | pet | | he |
| | too | **7** | will | | getting | | boy |
| | she | | out | | like | | be |
| | very | | guess | | it | **23** | we |
| | is | **8** | this | | here | | box |
| | a | | to | **13** | at | | play |
| | doll | **10** | little | | hello | **26** | was |
| | take | | house | | did | **29** | fun |
| | her | | eat(s) | | put | | |